Hey! Get Off Our Train

Hey! Get Off Our Train

John Burningham

CROWN PUBLISHERS, INC.

NEW YORK

For Chico Mendes
who tried so hard to protect the rain forest of Brazil

Published by Crown Publishers, Inc., a Random House company,
225 Park Avenue South, New York, New York 10003

CROWN is a trademark of Crown Publishers, Inc.

Originally published in Great Britain by Jonathan Cape Ltd., London,
in 1989.

First American Edition, 1990

Manufactured in the United States of America

2 3 4 5 6 7 8 9 10

Library of Congres Cataloging-in-Publication Data:
Burningham, John.
Hey! get off our train.
SUMMARY: At bedtime a young boy takes a trip on his toy train and
rescues several endangered animals.
ISBN: 0-517-57638-4 (trade); 0-517-57643-0 (lib. bdg.)
[1. Railroads—Trains—Fiction.   2. Rare animals—Fiction.
3. Bedtime—Fiction] I. Title.
PZ7.B936He   1989   [E]   89-15802

"You aren't still playing with that train are you?
Get into bed immediately. You know you have to be up
early for school tomorrow."

"Here is your pajama-case dog. I found it under a cushion in the sitting room. Now settle down and go to sleep."

"We're ready to go now.
Don't make too much noise with the shovel."

"If there's time, we can have a picnic."

"It looks as if it is going to be foggy ahead.
If it is, we can play ghosts."

"Hey! Get off our train."

"Please let me come with you on your train.
Someone is coming to cut off my tusks,
and soon there will be none of us left."

"It's going to be a very hot day.
If it is, we must find somewhere to go for a swim."

"Hey! Get off our train."

"Please let me come with you on your train.
If I stay in the sea, I won't have enough to eat,
because people are making the water very dirty
and they are catching too many fish,
and soon there will be none of us left."

"I think there is going to be a strong wind.
If there is, we can all fly kites."

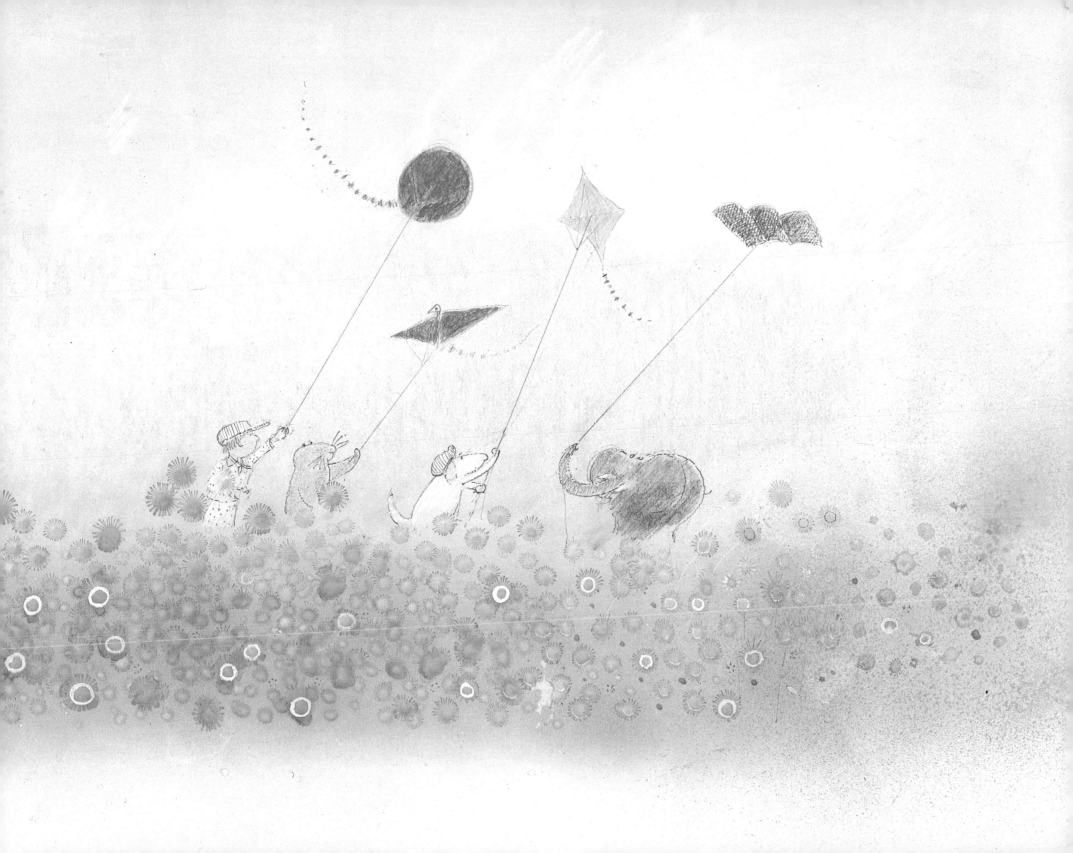

"Hey! Get off our train."

"Please let me come with you on your train.
I live in the marshes and they are draining
the water out of them. I can't live on dry land,
and soon there will be none of us left."

"It looks as if it is going to rain soon.
If it does, we can all muck about with umbrellas."

"Hey! Get off our train."

"Please let me come with you on your train.
They are cutting down the forests where I live,
and soon there will be none of us left."

"I think there's enough snow now.
If there is, we can all throw snowballs."

"Hey! Get off our train."

"Please let me ride on your train. I live in the frozen North
and somebody wants my fur to make a coat out of,
and soon there will be none of us left."

"If it does not stop snowing soon,
we are going to get stuck."

"We must go back now.
I have to go to school in the morning."

"You must get up immediately,
or you will be late for school.
There are lots of animals in the house.
There's an elephant in the hall,
a seal in the bathtub,
a crane in the laundry,
a tiger on the stairs,
and a polar bear by the fridge.
Does this have anything to do with you?"